for Grandpa Fred
—H.M.Z.

Text copyright © 2005 by Harriet Ziefert
Illustrations copyright © 2005 by Amanda Haley
All rights reserved / CIP Data is available.
Published in the United States by
🍎 Blue Apple Books
515 Valley Street, Maplewood, N.J. 07040
www.blueapplebooks.com
Distributed in the U.S. by Chronicle Books
First Edition
Printed in China
ISBN: 1-59354-076-0
1 3 5 7 9 10 8 6 4 2

40 USES
for a
GRANDPA

Harriet Ziefert

drawings by Amanda

BLUE APPLE BOOKS

1. play date

2. veterinarian

3. cash machine

4. taxi

5. e-pal

6. farmer

7. nurse

8. judge

9. mediator

10.
coach

11.
referee

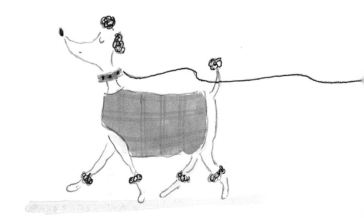

12. butler

13. pet minder

14. oarsman

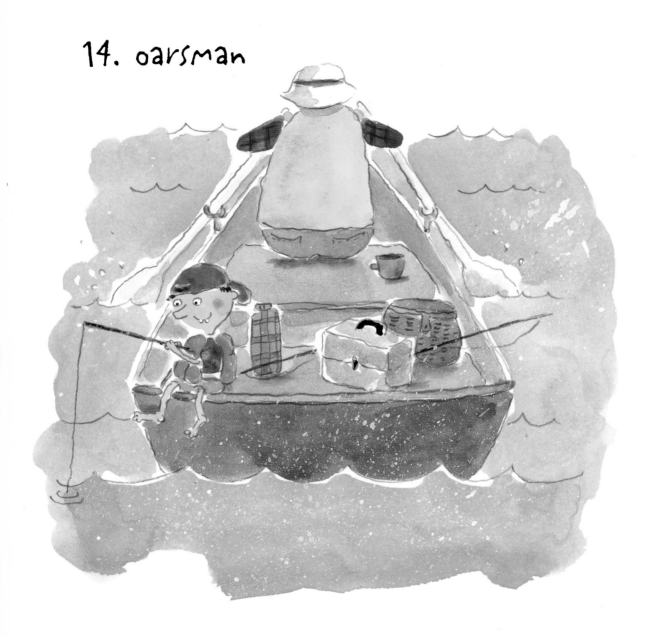

15.
dance partner

16. teacher

17. hand warmer

18. chef

19. entertainment center

20. cheerleader

21. flight attendant

22.
handyman

23. bug catcher

24.
architect

25. storyteller

26.
ticket
holder

27. shelf

28. photo album

29. partner

30. adding machine

31.
basketball
hoop

32. dictionary

33. tailor

34. baker

35. opponent

36.
valentine

37.
assistant

38.
toy maker

39. worm handler

40. Friend

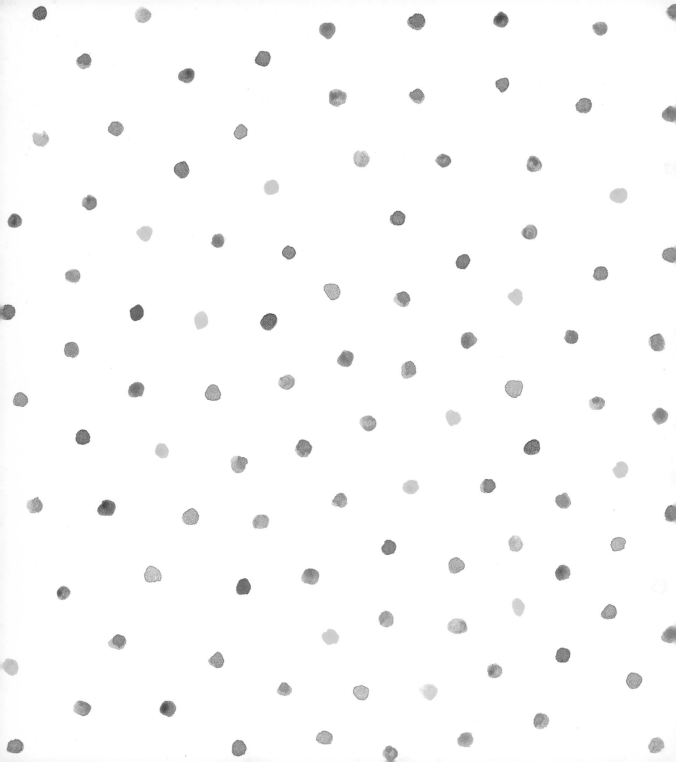